GW00731810

SDP
Sweat Drenched Press

Cover art by Laura-Jane Marshall
ISBN: 9798718737547

The Direction of

Greater Courage

Nicoletta Wylde

Index

BEFORE ME

Ramblin' Man

Can you throw the body out? or move it down, at least
It's just it's been three days my love and I'd quite like to sleep
That skeleton heart you nailed on the wall was gaining flesh and blood
But you cut my fingers through the gloves and told me not to touch

So honey what's the point of this goodbye if I don't **SHOUT**
It's just an easy way for you to find a clear path out
This corpse here it's been wailing since you declared the drought
Break my heart with maybe, break my heart *no doubt*

So you burn out our strange tapestries dismembered limbs inside
It's just intention forces demons deep into your mind
I'm ready to take this final breath, swim ruby butcher sea
And either way there was no need to be so cruel to me
either way there was no need to be so cruel to me

{inhale}

So I went and buried the body, covered it with sheets
and the thing about the Ramblin' Man - is that shit's all deceased
My skeleton heart I boiled the bones – cut off the flesh and blood
held new bold outstretched fingers, this prophet saving love

So firefly he taught me all there is and was to know
on taking risks that come by next and never lettin' go
our corpse reduced to worm's meat, and the fur tree squirrels sing
before the good strikes hard the bad, it's a karmic spin

So we both hand stitch new tapestries, I wear this heart with pride
it's just my magick sisters send frost visions as a guide
I watch your horse a ridin', dust flies overseas
new love crashes in like thunder, it's taking over me
brings new hope horizons, taking over me.

9-2-4

Do you dine on opium and hooch?
Back door trap door cat gets loose
You shouldn't have fucked with that board in your basement
So we talk of dive bars and astral displacement

Your place is *"embrace the knives in the sea"*
Tie rocks to my ankles
Don't take him from me
I think you could help and just hold my head down
I won't run to you – I'd rather just drown

Smooth talking jazz walking criminal mind
I should stop bugging you all of the time
Did you curse the heart I opted for?
Your call to arms; out of time metaphor

Your place is *"embrace the knives in the sea"*
Tie rocks to my ankles
Don't take him from me
I think you could help and just hold my head down
I won't run to you – I'd rather just drown

So I'm not leaving
I'm not leaving
I'm not leaving
I'm **NOT** leaving
I dream of your face in the dead of the night
Dreams don't overcome if there is no fright

Solve//Coagula

An elaborate scheme
But finally then
Stole my father's affliction
Through my mother's hands

Stained stars with sulphur
my vague new destiny
Solve my nest
Coagula take me
Maria says *"there's no use in feeling that shame!*
We still turn to lovers in times of pain."

&
Fool me not
I'm stronger than this
Anarchic clown
With her chainsaw kiss
But the snake is a circle
And the tail stops to say
Remains my choice - me being this way

Everyone Wants You With Me Except You

Kicking up parks and aching through towns
Begging you baby just come, get down
Breathing pollution, breathing smoke
Glances on stage, my fire, invoke

So I'm writing love letters,
What else can I do?
Everyone wants you with me except you

Obliterate this empty night
Songs from the city – songs to excite
Soldiers of soul mates, shattered past
You have no interest in winning my heart

So I'm writing love letters
What else can I do?
Everyone wants you with me except you

So I run with liars and beggars and thieves
All the sweet while my heart on my sleeve
I tell the foxes to cry of my plight
That I wish I could ask you to stay the night

So I'm writing love letters
What else can I do?
Everyone wants you with me except you

You blow me a kiss and my heart it beats fast
I swear these words might be the last
Yet I believe in love, truly, I do
Everyone wants you with me except you
Everyone wants you with me except you

About twelve? Maybe thirteen.

How many legs have I opened since you?
Circus tricks throughout the night
Kissed such flesh up against my own
Ached for a venomous bite

How many hands have I held since yours?
Whispered my secrets for Satan's sake
For a pound of sympathy my love
Mythology our own we make

But
I fancy you pace outside my window
Your voice catastrophic *(even in digital)*
And I fancy we're something
(twin souls!) (so unique!)
The Magus or even the Fool doth preach

{but/really}
it's just us
naked, pretend,
alone, and high,
confessing
our transgressive sin

Electric Light Canopy

A cavern of stars above my bed
you whispering in my dreams
I remember everything you said
time don't wear the seems

A cavern of stars above my head
time beats on in four by four
Etched the ground – slit my chest red
I never wanted you more

but I think of you and the nights get thicker
I think of you and the stars all flicker
I think of you and the candles burn slight
I think of you just to get through the night
I think of you and your sunken dreams
and timing timing timing sits between love and spleens

But my pride and the truth are worlds apart
"Just never give him he broke your heart."

Sedated

The truth of the fact can't be debated
I'm way nicer when I'm sedated
So hand me that drink with a chemical gown
To be honest I'm glad that it's me it took down

<u>As within so without</u>

Old lover quicksilver - kiss fast, hide my shame
I've done all my talking yet still I'm insane
Child of the earth and the starry sky
Regrets fall on deaf ears as Charon on slides
So hand me a drink from either lake
Cheers to Russian roulette, the inferno – **sedate**

Soar/Sore

365 days since we kissed
Something that I've rarely missed
pillow ash and my saving grace
was that I was never in your place (but)
The way that you stare and widen your eyes
Transcends all your bitter lies

365 since you said
We had to take cover – I've bleached out my head
I sing to the walls and to empty space
beg all the forces not to fall into place (but)
I still turn over in the dead of night
Swearing it's you I've been lying beside

You Call This Love

I was chasing the darkness man
I really made it move
Caught up in starlight with starshine at sunsets
Begging the big city to give me a ride
A bite
A sniff of that elixir of youth
Lord
Anything
From our glory days
Hazy Sundays
Hot dog hero days
Strung out singer days
Where bodies and bones and hearts broke way harder
Lurching around the big city with the lights in my eyes
cos I like the way the neon feels on my face
Yet

I feel like a ghost
And you call this love
but I say it's suicide
you call this love
it's your nature to generalise

I was chasing another guy
I really made him move
Following footsteps and footfalls with foot pain and fantasies
Bleaching confidence, parts of me that ached
with sickness
Lord
Something
will hit you
if you spend enough time outside

Neon flicker days
Growing weaker days
There's no way to make it quicker days

Still, I can't escape
that way the neon feels on my face

And I feel like a ghost.

Cos
You call this love
But I say it's suicide
Call you call this love
I swear, I never ever cried

Light {a solstice poem}

Up has down and day has night
I am just hidden from the light
Lilith I beg hold darkness tight
I am just hidden from the light
Accept from me an internal fight
I am just hidden from the light
So tear myself apart I might
I am just hidden from the light
To grow again anew a-bright
& fill what's left with celestial light
Balance then
just divine
rite?

Moving in the direction of greater courage

History is told by those who get old
But what do you do when old hearts grow mould?
So I burn out my future with you
You turned on the light in the middle of the night
But I got my fuel somewhere new

There used to be a time
I would have said my love was blind
it was you that made me this way
I never knew such deadly cold
Could escalate my heart's dissolve
Grab your coat and run away

You've got a subtle constitution (but I'm made of revolution)
breaking free made me this way
So your confession - eternal love
fall on deaf ears - snare your dove
So you see my dear I do not stay

But they never see these subtle shifts
They'll cock their head and say
We dine on destruction (we need it to function)
Girl, you'll fly right back someday
But truth be told if I weren't so cold
It would have been the same way

So cancel your bells and scrub out the names
Keep the preacher man in drink
Cos I'll tell you with spite in the middle of the night
It's not about you that I think

May I have one (1) crumb of Serotonin?!

Short skirt
eyes hurt
tell her
paralysed
I run for fun
You don't even try
So gold guild my heart
It won't be the same
Don't even like men
so why'd they drive me insane?

Mantra for Stoke Newington

We are the ones bread curious
We are the ones so furious
We are the ones that money won't fuel
We are the ones that deserved better schools

We dine on exquisite conversation
Your preference is not an approximation
of the life you had as a child
TV dinners, thighs defiled

White wine spritzer
Crystal glass
I am not this middle class

We are the ones with broken homes
We are the ones who can't get loans
We are the ones who'll fall all our way
We are the ones who'll live for today

We dine on exquisite conversation
Your preference is not an approximation
of the life you had as a child
TV dinners, thighs defiled

White wine spritzer
Crystal glass
I am not this middle class

<u>Life in Widescreen</u>

Cigarette holes say change the scene
House lights low, analogue beam
You're the sweetest thing I've ever seen
Life in widescreen, life in widescreen

Guided by a vivid dream
My heart was bleeding - *men are mean*
You suture it up **(keep your needles clean)**
Life in widescreen, life in widescreen

So I don't care if we seem too keen
I don't like the apathy scheme
Push me down on all fours, your beauty queen
Life in widescreen, life in widescreen

Mary-Ann

Oh Mary-Ann you bitter thing
He won't give you anything
You'll twist and turn in Lucifer's shadow
And you don't think that I can handle
Prickly aniseed bitter words
Things I'll swear you never heard
Taken as gospel on parchment page
I will never show my rage (but)
Part the skies and drain the river
Just to watch your body quiver

Now I leave him to decide
So I leave this with my pride
His body snow clad perfect white
Face in my hands for a few lonely nights
I keep the moments you'll never see
Cos Mary-Ann his ghost loves me

Ellipses

You promised me I was your Princess
but it's midnight and I'm the dispossessed
I guess sometime
I oughta be leaving
Cos you don't change your spots
is what I'm perceiving

Madhouse Ashes

I read what you wrote
whilst I was sleeping
charcoal jasmine
third-eye smoke
my eyes, your eyes, our eyes
they always betray us
if I could choose
I'd feed them to that legendary crow
a hundred times
before mine are yours
but
you take them without asking
anyway

so what are you gonna do
when
they catch you in the fire
there's only so much
that the burn ward can do
lover
with all your smarts
you'd better start thinkin' **fast**

yet
somewhere
inside all this
you smile
despite it all
and say
baby
I can't work in that madhouse
any more
which is funny
(I think)
cos
you drive me crazy

Heavy rain on the 22:41 at Kings X

My love I ain't been a saint I know
I'm more inclined to bed those wild
But it's about groundwork
about taking note
Red margin marks
All you said and wrote

My love I promise it's all fair play
I'm allied with the moon
You ain't about labels
You're about the game
Grass mowed
Paint lain

(just inhale fuck, please just inhale)

Cos I never declared the battleground
On account you ain't started the war
But you best believe I'm changing my round
if they win the fight, I'll have your war

So the noise of the rain on the station
speaks in tongues and just for me
Changed whilst I waded the ocean
But you found me lurking by the sea

So this could be the storm on any damn train
One of those cities with a stupid ass name
I've danced through the rain - now I'm wet
Won favours from a rain Gods
so now I bet

You'll sing me love songs you've never spoken
I'm drenched, your lost
I'm healed, you're broken

Violence

Babe, my life is violence
Violence
So I'm just panicking is all
I'll keep silent

So give me the codeine
Pass me the liquor
Please just make this season go quicker

Torn apart

They're as flippant as the wind, the sheet thin ice
Yet in my company they make nice
I try so hard to reconnect
so maybe our threads won't detangle yet
But I know she's been talking
& I don't know what she told them
My heart just recognised love long left
Thus they exclude and leave me bereft

So tell me how it feels to be black marked
To be torn apart
How can I explain how it feels to be black marked
Tear it all apart
An enforced brand-new start

He's standing there in his ice king glory
Coming up with another story
I try so hard to keep it polite
To engage and ignore all the previous bite
But I know they've been talking
I'll guess what they've told him
Ice heart restart not everyone knows
The effects of what we both chose

So tell me how it feels to be black marked
To be torn apart
How can I explain how it feels to be black marked
Tear it all apart
my enforced brand-new start

BEHIND ME

Fillin' in Rabbit Holes with Rubble

Except for the night
It's another new life
Another lady sayin' I ain't sick
But the fact of it all is when it's dark my dreams fall
Down a road that just makes me feel sick
So since that final day
You went away
I've closed my doors
lighthouse locked
Intoxication so wrong
I never got to be strong
So you bet I'm movin' on

So feed your needle tooth bitches
Just give 'em their prey
Till you realise it's you that made them this way
So I'm filling what's left of the rabbit holes with rubble
Thus **remains** my choice to stay out of trouble

Except for one rat
It was a clear path back
Another anecdote *"I got too deep"*
But the fact of it all is my heart it did fall
For someone else that satisfies its peak
So 'though your needle scars ache Doll
it sure don't replace
What I built
plans re-laid
Intoxication all gone
No more opium song
So daydream I'm just movin' on

So feed your needle tooth bitches
Just give 'em their prey
Till you realise it's you that made them this way
So I'm filling what's left of the rabbit holes with rubble

Thus **remains** my choice to stay out of trouble

Microscopic Ego

In every corner I place your name
& the streets they speak the same
As the moment when you turned and you said
Will they rent us an hour on a bed

But I called your bluff
And it was just enough
And I'll rejoice the same
at the fact that demon's slain

And it's over
{come dance with my microscopic ego}
And we're sober
{take a chance with my microscopic ego}
Although the streets they scream your name
It's just the memory of your game
I built a pyre gone out to sea
So you don't get the best of me
Or the rest of me

So the heart you played with first
Never satisfied its thirst
From the night I spun the sacrament
I ate my heart and I was content

But I called your bluff
And it was just enough
And I'll rejoice the same
at the fact that demon's slain

And it's over
{come dance with my microscopic ego}
And we're sober
{no romance for my microscopic ego}
And it's over
And we're sober

Although the streets they scream your name
It's just the memory of your game
I built a pyre gone out to sea
You won't get the best of me
Or the rest of me
Or the rest of me

But I called your bluff
And it was just enough
And I'll rejoice the same
at the fact that demon's slain

take a chance take a chance take a chance
no romance no romance no romance
no romance no romance no romance
no romance no romance no romance
no romance no romance no romance
no romance no romance no romance
no romance no romance no romance
no romance no romance no romance

Won't fight anymore

She brings the dark weather
The flickering change
Swirls of spittle and wolfs bane
She says I know they've taught your magic is bad
But that is not the choice that I had

And I know I know I know dear one
I have to make this right
I know I know I know my love, you've got to find your fight

But I know she tries
and she delights in the truth and the light
and she's sure

But the sun has gone dark
& I've been surpassed
I just can't fight any more
Won't fight no more

She brings tide in November
The tedious part
Teardrops of energy shaken apart
She says I know I know I know they'll teach you what to say
But you are not
You are not
the cards that they'll lay

And I know I know I know dear one
I have to make this right
I know I know I know my love, you've got to find your fight

But I know she tries
and she delights in the truth and the light
and she's sure

But the sun has gone dark

& I’ve been surpassed
I just can't fight any more
Won't fight no more

Magick Sisters

Come precious flowers
Summer's our hour
Come careful creatures
We'll be your teachers
Come precious forest
and offer your tallest
Come magick sisters
Dance with your misters
Come darling branches
With power your arches
Fold over girls with the wind in their hair
Gold in their teeth, caught in fates snare
Who talk to birds and briars and beasts
Ache to bring forth your monthly feast

Sexually receptive

Oh sister I'm sorry
I just lied
But the thought leaves me broken
just paralysed
but I've been through the game where my terrible art
tears relationships and families apart

So what's between my thighs
I'm sanitised
Crawl beneath goodbyes
I'm sanitised
Crave out my insides
Just sanitised
but I am alive

Oh brother don't hate me
Way too long
Since you happened to ask how my day has gone
and I've been through the game where I spit out my heart
Remember? It's me who stitched up the parts

So what's between my thighs
I'm sanitised
Crawl beneath goodbyes
I'm sanitised
Crave out my insides
Just sanitised
but I am alive

I wrote a hundred times

The echo of the love of my life through darkness
Fire-tinged sequin un-matching shoes
blead tap tap tap on my heartstrings
dust aching through my fingers
The echo sail idol off into the darkness

{preaching}

unholy sermons and blasphemous half-reasons
that this was the best thing for it

bind my hands with good intention
false promises
and whispers of what if
and maybe
and probably
and one day
taste like stale beer and foreign tobacco
and could have
tastes like bile in my chest
and maybe
tastes like sunrise when I haven't slept

I've got too much faith in what's meant to come back,
but he shivered away – anyway

I wrote a hundred times
Things I felt like I should say
But he stumbled on his lines
he doesn't love me anyway

Poetry

No one cares about your poetry
Weren't even here till I was 23
So here's a poem for those with robbed adolescence
and monstrous hearts we work to silence

No one cares about your poetry
They only talk about mental harmony
So button up my girl give them a show
Just as it happened oh so long ago

Don't write you off, love
Keep being soft, love
And still remember you're catching up
remember that your here cause of more than just luck

Don't write you off, love
Keep being soft, love
And still remember you're catching up
you are just here cause of more than just luck

I'm not dying, I'm transcending

You promised me you'd never leave
this you said was guaranteed
and then you left me all alone
to face such fears upon my own

So they got to you
they got they got
They got to you
They got they got
Everyone thinks she's oh so nice
But I transcend her bitter life

& I have to accept that you left me bereft
It's not what I wanted to be
but the truth of the fact is you don't give back
and you don't want to talk to me
talk to me

You promised me a new kind of love
Sisterhood and stars above
Serotonin & MDMA
Won't it always be this way?

So they got to you
they got they got
They got to you
They got they got
Everyone thinks she's oh so nice
But I transcend her bitter life

& I have to accept that you left me bereft
It's not what I wanted to be
but the truth of the fact is you don't give back
and you don't want to talk to me
talk to me

{SO}
Pull my knees off the floor
Skewer my ribs inside
I've made it way too far to pray
You won't even tell me why

When

It's not a case of maybe
It's just case of when
Scissors as good as knives
Whilst ligatures my friend
And you know it makes so much sense
To burn out bright
as fame intends
My version that suffers is oh so done
So hang my body on meat hooks
give my soul another one
I'm tired of paralysis, hunger, the tram
So It's not a case of maybe
Just a case of when

N-R-E

You left me with a kiss
Infected / half dying
Shadows of our love making
{Points gained there for trying}
All consume so I eat nothing
To use a metaphor
Hand prints across my chest
Babe, do you want more?
We speak of secret things
Chemistry and the weather
The city is ours for the taking
So let's burn it down together

But I'm not in love
It's not even a crush
I'm just looking for a way to gush
Twist me bite me hit me hard
Take the lead baby you're in charge
Work my body so I see the result
You're the high priest in my cult
I'm not in love
It's only a crush
So I'm begging you begging you make me blush

Mercy

Oh mercy mercy let me live again
Pluck out a star and change my fate
Your love song it comes out of the blue
Way too fast and way too late

And I might fancy it was for me
But the truth has already been told
And in the end the fool was me
So don't say hi - stay uninvolved

ON MY LEFT HAND

Hush

Hush little baby don't say a word
Daddy's gonna chase that thing you heard
And if that thing you heard don't stick
Daddy's gonna give you a fingertip
And if that fingertip don't last
Daddy's gonna pick you up from class
And if that post class ride chat don't sting
Daddies gonna make you his everything

Now hush little baby don't say a word
Daddy's gonna cut your mum up first
And if that cutting out don't sting
Daddy's gonna lie about everything
And if that everything is sad
Daddy's gonna buy a gift that's rad
And if that gift your heart don't buy
Daddy's gonna mimic nights gone buy

Now hush little baby don't say a word
Never mind that noise you heard
Hush little baby don't get it right
No way now he's gonna hurt you at night
Hush little baby, calm your smite
He's my Dad, he'd never do that, right?!

Madhouse

I read what you wrote
whilst I was sleeping
soundtrack
you tip tip tapping
away
on your type writer
that you use
cos
you think I find it romantic
except I think it just makes you look
like a prick

because I'm not as moral
as I think I am
I read what you wrote
about me being the fire
yet
you don't mind when I burn you
and my eyes, my eyes, my eyes
they always betray me
if I could choose
I'd feed them to the crows a hundred times
before
they are yours
to put in a poem
but
you take them without asking
anyway

so you tell me not to talk about it
but what are we gonna do
when
they see your fire scars
there's only so much that
the burn ward can do
lover

with all your smarts
you'd better start thinkin' fast

& somewhere
in between all this
you smile and say
baby
I can't work in that madhouse
any more
which is funny
(I think)
cos
you drive me crazy

If you must go

I ambled our Charon highway
This two-day pass and a whisky flask
strangers' fingerprints; unknown implements
Looking to get outta my head for a while
Say you'll pull me right outta my bed for a while
Don't ya know you gotta watch out for them embers honey
Cos you gonna get yourself burnt

So if you must go
If you have to go
When you must go
Just wait for the snow
So I can follow
(If you'll let me follow)

I trampled our Charon highway
light strands and handstands
Unknown paths; danger smarts
All looking for a way to get laid for a while
Say your ghost might stay for a while
so maybe I like the way the flesh smells
Is why I'm sizzling my seashells
Grass-stain heart, electricity smart, steal a cigarette and blow

So if you must go
If you have to go
When you must go
Just wait for the snow
So I can follow
(If you'll let me follow)

Chasing her Sparkle

That much serotonin makes me sick
So swallow down the water quick
Cos
Whilst I was over there watching the light show
You were out the back door chasing her sparkle

And I don't know if it is enough
To be tiny and beautiful
but come unstuck
When it comes to the time to pay our rent
Pennies for our thoughts
yet nothing to spend

I'm asking no more than a
Lift round the corner
It's not like I need the whole drain
I can't get unstuck and medicine star struck
Replaces my blood with champagne
But the benzos are in there
Not-right kind of self-care
& I know you'll be mad about that
Be mad 'bout that

And I don't know if it's enough
I'm terrified they'll call my bluff
When it comes to the time to confess my sin
They'll find out I let the devil right in

Fuck heart

He came from outer-space he had nothing to lose
Cupid hair and snake print shoes
And he started all the rumours that she might bite
Utterly intrenched in her need to fight
She'll say:
"You misrepresent my confidence
And you might have me down with no defence
You don't see my inner might
All I know is fire and smite"

Her sharp points so hard to touch
He don't like that shape too much
Her sharp points so hard to touch
He don't like that shape too much

Fuck heart - stand still
Then he's easier to kill
Fuck heart - stand still
Then he's easier to kill

So she brings the dark whether and flickering change
Swirls of spittle and wolfsbane
But she might be the alchemist to make his night
Utterly intrenched in her opiate-life
She'll say:
"You misrepresent my confidence
And you might have me down with no defence
You, don't see my inner might
All I know is fire and smite"

Her sharp points so hard to touch
He don't like that shape too much
Her sharp points so hard to touch
He don't like that shape too much

{pause}

Fuck heart - stand still
Then he's easier to kill
Fuck heart - stand still
Then he's easier to kill

Light me up

Light me up
Eat this pyre
My desire can inspire
I dreamt your heart
Was made of wire
This desire took me higher
To fill that hole
Fuck prophecy scryer
It's nothing more
than our night as a liar

ON MY RIGHT HAND

White Noise

We called each other names from each sides of the channel
white noise I’m in deep
white noise I can’t handle
Surprised I still miss your crisis apparition
So map out my veins, inject your condition

Holy Cup

You pacified me with a holy cup
Laced with blood and poison
You never thought I might stop to lap
the art behind your treason

But I drunk till my limbs ached
Holding onto the bile
Spat it into someone's face
Well healing, it does take a while

Then he got sick – you ran away
And I got happy – then you got laid
Then I messed with art and you with magick
and you with force and I with habit

I cut your cup into five pieces
Bound with my bleeding chord
Waited till the storm had receded
Smashed my boat down on the shore

Then I opened the door of someone's heart
and what I found inside
Broke my brain reset my path
Bile and blood to shadows and blind

(I don't know which is better, and I don't know which is better)

Wayward feet

Once you said that she was pretty
But she's three sizes bigger
And made of infamy
So I'm made of bones and ash and hate
I know I know I should raise you up
But I think it's too late
So I rehearse in great symphony
something between you
some heatstroke of infamy
fuck
I knew you had it in for me

Hiroshima

Hiroshima's in my head again
We meet each night on the astral plane
He needs to explode to feel the effect
Consequence around for days
So: -
I'm too small to force my point
And I need only fact
It's Oppenheimer next exploit
your kisses send me mad

Ideation

You say it's a good thing
I'm planning new looks
My new adoration
Keep busy! - it works
But really?
The reason I made this space fit me?
I just want somewhere to die that's like...pretty

Invocation of the brother of death

Lonely warriors of astral plane
As darkness falls we meet again
creep cracks in my windows, creep gaps in my doors
Gather here, your nightly cause

Lonely warriors of astral plane
I offer sleep starved arms to chain
and never were their ropes so sweet
as the ones you tie round my arms, my feet

Lonely warriors of astral plane
spectres of darkness, hearts profane
the part that scars my mind the most
their Priest he writhes on the chest of the host

Lonely warriors of astral plane
there was no time before your reign
when you held me in my younger years
the ghosts! I'd gasp, the ghosts are here!

Lonely warriors of astral plane
pillars of shadow, lords of disdain
Cloaks they shield such gleeful eyes
Their whispers laugh out my demise

Lonely warriors of astral plane
Choke hard, choke deep, choke till I'm slain
A lover's smother, it ain't as pure
As the fight you gathered round me for

Lonely warriors of astral plane
I beg you someone please explain
terror footsteps - the doctor she said
it's way more, my darling, than just in your head

Sky Spirit Confession

[you never left me//you never left me//I left you//I left you]

He is the dead
he comes at night
hair caught in my fairy lights
darkness preach dislocated noise
thickened whispers – imposter voice

He is the dead
he stops when I start
wild horses his ace card
veil drops on the stage
of devilry, those eyes – my rage

He is the dead
shakes hearts apart
and sure I know he looks real smart
and I never quite know how to say
'that dance pushed faithful lips away
I only want you for one night
all that is inside my sight
to fuck and nip and sigh and groan
kiss me quick, leave me alone
birth the beast for just one bite
oh darling – I don't want to treat you right

[Goodbye!! *laugh* Goodbye!!]

My lovers have left me

My lovers have left me
In one way or another
It's hard but they find better options
Discover
Someone less painful
More silent
Mature
Someone who will not push them for more
My problem of course is I see potential
And they see my body as just short rental

Phantombit

O lord
You really had it made
Sitting there on your throne of cocaine
Hidden blade for the cutting smile
This beauty queen on your scene for a while

So take me on down to that dusty old road
Bleed blue danger and heaviest load
Count it out in fallen hair
bleached the pure colour
genetic flair
Pause the clock and let me sit
red and black flowers in bouquet split
Roses, posies, please admit
Roses, posies, phantombit

O lord
Now I'm left quite insane
Calling on out to another dark shape
preen feathered dreams for the shortest while
Six hundred mg & my brains back in style

So take me on down to that dusty old road
Bleed blue danger and heaviest load
Count it out in fallen hair
bleached the pure colour
genetic flair
Pause the clock and let me sit
red and black flowers in bouquet split
Rosie's, posies, please admit
Rosie's posies phantombit

I am the victim
I am the victim
I am the victim
I am the victim

Long game

My love I ain't been a saint I know
I'm more inclined to bed the devil
But it's about timing
My love
You'll say
Breathing in coffee, chip my ice away

My love I admit it was him more than you
For a short while - for a short while
But it's about groundwork
My love
taking note
Everything you ever said and wrote

Cos I never declared this a battleground
On account you ain't started the war
But you best believe I'm just changing my round
She wins the battle – I'll get your all

{this is a fairytale}

I dreamed a scene this fairytale
Where they'd taken a knife and sliced out my fat
And we walk, hand in hand and I am not frail
I don't know what I'd say to that

No secret gene, no smashed genetics
No crossed wire brain, no anaesthetic
No forgotten name, no pragmatic tact
Not even insane, no not even that

I dreamed a scene this, a fairytale
Don't put your belief into anything packed
And we walk, hand in hand and the sunrise won't fail
But I don't know what I'd say to that

For before me flames the pentagram

& behind me shines the six-rayed star

So mote it be.

SDP
Sweat Drenched Press

Printed in Great Britain
by Amazon